Top 10 Romance of 2012, 2015, and 2016.

— BOOKLIST: THE NIGHT IS MINE, HOT POINT,
HEART STRIKE

One of our favorite authors.

— RT BOOK REVIEWS

Buchman has catapulted his way to the top tier of my favorite authors.

— FRESH FICTION

A favorite author of mine. I'll read anything that carries his name, no questions asked. Meet your new favorite author!

— THE SASSY BOOKSTER, FLASH OF FIRE

M.L. Buchman is guaranteed to get me lost in a good story.

— THE READING CAFE, WAY OF THE WARRIOR:
NSDQ

I love Buchman's writing. His vivid descriptions bring
everything to life in an unforgettable way.

— PURE JONEL, HOT POINT

KEE'S WEDDING

A NIGHT STALKERS WEDDING STORY

M. L. BUCHMAN

Buchman Bookworks

Other works by M. L. Buchman:

The Night Stalkers
Main Flight
The Night Is Mine
I Own the Dawn
Wait Until Dark
Take Over at Midnight
Light Up the Night
Bring On the Dusk
By Break of Day
White House Holiday
Daniel's Christmas
Frank's Independence Day
Peter's Christmas
Zachary's Christmas
Roy's Independence Day
Damien's Christmas
and the Navy
Christmas at Steel Beach
Christmas at Peleliu Cove
5E
Target of the Heart
Target Lock on Love
Target of Mine

Firehawks
Main Flight
Pure Heat
Full Blaze
Hot Point
Flash of Fire
Wild Fire
Smokejumpers
Wildfire at Dawn
Wildfire at Larch Creek
Wildfire on the Skagit

Delta Force
Target Engaged
Heart Strike
Wild Justice

Where Dreams
Where Dreams are Born
Where Dreams Reside
Where Dreams Are of Christmas
Where Dreams Unfold
Where Dreams Are Written

Eagle Cove
Return to Eagle Cove
Recipe for Eagle Cove
Longing for Eagle Cove
Keepsake for Eagle Cove

Henderson's Ranch
Nathan's Big Sky

Love Abroad
Heart of the Cotswolds: England

Dead Chef Thrillers
Swap Out!
One Chef!
Two Chef!

Deities Anonymous
Cookbook from Hell: Reheated
Saviors 101

SF/F Titles
The Nara Reaction
Monk's Maze
the Me and Elsie Chronicles

Strategies for Success (NF)
Managing Your Inner Artist/Writer
Estate Planning for Authors

5 YEARS AGO

The events in this story occur before the last scene of
I Own the Dawn
(The Night Stalkers #2).

"What if I'm not ready?"

"Since when haven't you been ready for anything?"

"This is different!" Kee Smith shouted her protest over the DAP Hawk helicopter's intercom.

Major Emily Beale did one of her magic tricks, slewing the helo around in a way that no other pilot possibly could. It gave Kee—perched at the side-gunner crew chief's position, close behind the copilot's seat—a clear shot on the lead vehicle in the column racing across the nighttime Afghan desert.

Kee grabbed the double handles on her M134 minigun, slid it out the window to the limit of the stops, and pulled the trigger. In answer, the electric motor spun the six-barrel Gatling gun up to five hundred rpm. The stream of 7.62mm ammunition raced out of the case, through the delinker, and into each barrel's chamber at precisely the right moment. She sent three thousand rounds per minute raking down out of the darkness. Every tenth round was an infrared tracer, brilliant green in her own night-vision gear—yet effectively invisible to anyone not so equipped.

Her first rounds struck less than ten meters in front of the lead vehicle, so she held steady and let the lead vehicle drive right into the hail of bullets. *Su-weet!* A practiced shake allowed her to destroy the engine. The truck lurched sideways off the road and slammed to a halt in the deep sand.

The copilot fired a Hydra 70 rocket to take out the anti-aircraft gun mounted on the truck bed as Kee continued to slice up the line of vehicles. Two RPGs were fired upwards, but in no particular direction and were no threat to their flight of four blacked-out helicopters. The Night Stalkers of the US Army's 160th SOAR ruled the night.

A Little Bird flying close beneath them took out the beater Toyota Corolla that had been the source of the RPGs as Kee and her fellow gunner Big John kept the convoy trapped on the road and behind the now-burning lead vehicle.

Big John was wisely staying out of this conversation. But if he so much as laughed, he'd be dead meat the moment they were back on the ground. She'd pulverize him herself, even if he was twice her size.

"I am so-o-o not ready for this shit!" Kee unleashed another chain of destruction on a captured Humvee. She must have managed to punch into some ammo cache through the turret gunner's position as the vehicle flared brightly inside, then exploded violently as they flew over it and raced once more into the desert.

"If I can do it, so can you," Emily replied with no real hint of sympathy as she rolled the Black Hawk completely over and somehow managed to come out of the maneuver headed back toward the column.

"But you're the legendary Major Emily Beale. I'm just

Sergeant Kee Smith. I'm not even that—I made up my last name."

"Get your act together, Kee," Major Beale sighed. "Night Stalkers Don't Quit!"

Having the motto of the 160th SOAR thrown in her face wasn't helping one bit. As to getting her shit together...since when was that even a possibility.

Emily certainly had though. She and Major Henderson had been married six months and still they walked about as if on some freaking honeymoon.

The MH-60M DAP Hawk banked hard, giving Kee a straight-down view on the militia's column. She unleashed more mayhem on them with her minigun.

This she could handle.

Her own wedding to Archie? In less than seventy-two hours? Not so much.

CHAPTER 2

Captain Archibald Stevenson III, lay on the Italian beach and wondered how this had come to be his world. More accurately, he lay *in* the beach. His soon-to-be-adopted daughter, Dilya, had spent the last hour steadily covering him with a thick layer of sand until it lay on his chest like a lead blanket. It had been scorching hot at first with the Mediterranean sun beating down on him. Now that he was deeper under the sand there was a pleasant coolness to it.

Thankfully, pre-burial, he had pulled his hat low against the mid-morning sun. Dilya had made him promise not to peek, but he'd squinted out at her a few times anyway to make sure she was okay.

The eleven- or twelve-year-old Uzbekistani orphan—even she wasn't sure—appeared completely content as she worked some artistic magic with a bright blue plastic shovel the size of his palm. Kee had rescued the starving waif from a frigid mountaintop deep in a war zone barely three months ago. Now, in just three more days when he married Kee, the three of them would become the most unlikely family imaginable.

Despite her constantly prodigious appetite, Dilya was still pencil thin, though no longer gaunt. She'd been little more than a ragged ghost at first—and as flighty as one, disappearing at the least alarm. She'd settled into herself in surprising ways and proven herself highly adaptable. First at Forward Operating Base Bati where he and Kee had been stationed, then back in the States with him and his parents after he'd been shot and had to have his shoulder replaced.

The two of them had seen Kee only briefly during these last three months, but the transformation between them had been nothing short of miraculous. Archie loved Dilya, with her long, dark hair and mystical green eyes, and had no doubt that she loved him back. But the connection between Dilya and Kee was closer than he'd ever imagined a mother and daughter could be—though one was born of Uzbek refugees and the other on the streets of East L.A.

Kee.

Archie resisted the urge to itch at the sand which had now penetrated every single pore. Dilya had been very exasperated at the damage to her artwork when he'd done so earlier. He tried focusing on the soft lapping of the Mediterranean waves, the soft lilt of Italian among other families enjoying the sunny morning, even the laughter of their children—but all he could think about was the itchy sand.

Kee was an even bigger puzzle than Dilya. How had she slipped into his heart so completely? She was feisty, obnoxious, tough-as-nails, and an amazing soldier. Her permanently dark tan skin, Asian narrow eyes, and exceptionally curved body had made her a fantasy to look at. Even her dark hair with its saucy little blonde-dyed strip had been cute as hell.

There was a dark side to her as well, that she'd revealed to him in her typical manner—a single, massive emotional blast. One moment she'd been this sexy companion who he couldn't get enough of, and the next she'd been the miracle proof of what could be done by pure willpower. Everything about her had a deeper meaning, even the little stripe of golden hair.

There had never been a woman like her!

Whenever they were apart, he wondered how he could be with someone from such a different world. His parents were upper crust Boston and Mom was a top strategic consultant to the White House on global geopolitics. He himself was a top ten West Point grad. Kee had finished high school by getting her GED before becoming an Army infantry grunt and working her way up to being a Night Stalker.

There was no way the three of them should work well as a unit.

Yet whenever they were together, his mismatched family-to-be made absolute perfect sense. Kee was so damned… alive! It made him wonder what she saw in him. Not that he was complaining, but it made him wonder.

"Soon, Dilya. Soon we will all be back together."

The slight girl barely nodded as she focused on her sandy creation. Then she glanced at his face. "I say no peekings. *Ha?*" *Yes?* in Uzbek.

"No peekings. *Ha.*" He didn't bother to correct her *peekings* and simply closed his eyes once more. Her English was improving fantastically—with the help of nightly doses of *Winnie the Pooh* or *Charlotte's Web*—far faster than he'd ever done with a foreign tongue, but she must be sick of the constant little corrections. Time to give the kid a break.

Archie wasn't sure which of them he was reassuring anyway. The doctors had signed off on his recovery. His shoulder was as good as new—almost. He'd never be able to fly to 160th SOAR standards again, but that was the only real limitation.

But without flying, his future was a complete unknown. Too many options.

His mother wanted him to return to D.C. and work with her consulting firm. She'd spent much of last night working to convince him she was right, and almost had.

The Army wanted to slot him into mission planning at the Pentagon.

Or maybe he needed to break away. Be out on his own, doing who knew what.

But he wasn't on his own.

He'd promised that in three days he'd be saying *yes* to being a family. A family was meant to be together, not scattered across the planet. For three months he'd sought an answer, but been stumped every time.

If he couldn't fly… But no answer lay on the other side of that question.

Soon they'd be back together, he'd reassured Dilya.

But would they? He'd met Kee on her first day with the Night Stalkers just four months ago. She'd barely started in this phase of her military career when his future with the Night Stalkers had been taken away by a gunshot wound. There was no future for them. Getting married made no sense whatso—

"You look now."

"You *can* look now," then he bit his tongue. So much for giving Dilya a language break.

"You *can* look now. You can *look* now. You can look…" Dilya whispered variations to herself as she integrated the correction into her understanding of English.

And what would part of being a fractured family would be good for her?

Maybe he should walk away while he still could.

Do what was right for them.

He opened his eyes and squinted against the brightness. His parents, who had picked up the burden of caring for him and Dilya these last months, had flown out for the wedding last night. They'd been sleeping in, so he'd left a note where they could find him and Dilya on the beach. Now they were standing by his feet and looking down at him with slightly confused smiles. They often didn't understand Dilya's curiously mashed-up view of her past culture colliding with her new exposure to America, but loved her like a grandchild nonetheless. Kee they were far less sure about.

Archie tipped his head up to try and see, but the sand covering his body all of the way to his neck stopped him. So much sand that he couldn't sit up really. He pushed a little harder, but his new shoulder twinged and he dropped back down to rest his head on the beach. Three months to full range of motion, but another six months or more until it would be back up to full strength. Light duty only.

Dilya looked panicked, turning between him and her sand creation, only now understanding that he was in no position to see what she had spent most of the morning building.

Taking pity on him, Dad snapped a photo with his phone and then came to hold it where Archie could see it.

Archie saw what it was right away.

Laying on her side atop his chest, was a half-size version of Kee. And curled in her arms was a half-Dilya-sized figure. A pair of powerful arms made of sand sprouted from where his shoulders were buried beneath the sand. They cradled both the woman and girl lying upon his chest.

Archie had always seen Kee as the anchor of their new family because she was such a force of nature.

But that's not how Dilya saw it.

She saw him.

"Oh, Dilya."

Her expression was carefully devoid of emotion. But he could see the sunlight catching the watery brightness in her green eyes. A girl who had lost so much looked at him—at *him*—with tears of hope. How could he deny that?

"*Ha.* Dilya. Very *ha.*"

"Not gonna be catching this boy doing anything that kind of crazy," Big John declared as he thumped his dinner tray on the mess tent's table.

The place was buzzing after last night's successful attack. It jazzed up the whole camp, even the people who hadn't been along for the ride. The small team of Delta Force operators were quiet in their corner, of course, but the 75th Rangers were talking it up as if it had been their own mission.

Majors Beale and Henderson were doing their usual table-for-two off to one side so as not to impose their command presence on the rest of the team's celebratory mood.

"Doing what kind of crazy?" Kee asked because it was expected, but kept an eye on the majors. She'd tried picturing herself in their shoes: she and Archie. Content to simply sit together over a meal. But she could never make it happen in her head. The majors were the perfect couple. The two most decorated Night Stalker pilots in any battalion. Both beautiful, Mark poster-boy handsome and Emily magazine-ad blonde. Both so assured of their place in the world.

That could never be her.

Then she spotted that Emily had a single foot forward under the table, the sole of her boot resting on the toe of Henderson's. It made them human and *that* she could almost imagine…just not for someone like her.

"That's some crazy-ass shit you're gonna be doing," John was digging into a massive serving of pasta slathered with red sauce, pesto, and a fistful of Parmesan.

"It's me," she turned her attention back to her own meal. "Crazy shit is what I do. What are you talking about this time?" She spun a forkful of spaghetti and stuffed it in her mouth.

"'Bout you getting married, Smith."

Kee almost choked.

"That's way the hell outside the mission profile," Crazy Tim agreed as he dropped into the seat across from her, then reached across and stole a slice of garlic bread even though he had several of his own.

She casually reached over and took his apple pie before "accidentally" dumping his glass of milk in the tray.

Tim didn't even blink as he fished his fork out of the white puddle swirling around the bottom of his plate, licked it off, and began eating. He ignored the milk pool as if it was just a decoration.

"We like Archie and all, but marriage?" Tim mumbled around a big bite of Kee's stolen garlic bread. "Seriously, Smith, what's up with that? Is that how someone gets a woman to say *I do*? Gets his shoulder shot up and you go all swoony for him?"

Big John clasped his huge hands together, tucked them under his chin, and fluttered his eyelashes at her. Six-four of towering black man swooning like a little girl was too much and actually earned him a laugh. For a reward she gave him Tim's slice of apple pie. She desperately needed to laugh.

When it was someone like Archie, who had kept fighting beside her until the mission was complete *after* having his shoulder shot up, it definitely did count. When he played so sweetly with Dilya, or called Kee herself "Helen of Troy" for being sexy enough to launch a thousand ships, that counted to.

The rest of the crew from the majors' two DAP Hawks landed farther down the table, but they were much more concerned with reliving the mission, so she ignored them. Connie, the quiet new mechanic, veered aside and sat off at a table by herself. She was turning out to be an okay person, but Kee didn't have time to think about her at the moment. Maybe after Kee was back from her honeymoon.

Her *honeymoon?*

Shit! Since when was she the sort of person that would ever have one of those?

"Just between two gunners," Big John leaned down and whispered softly while Tim was busy trying to steal Dusty's soda to replace his own spilled milk, "I think Archie is one of the luckiest shits anywhere, Kee. You're hot as they get and you totally kick ass."

Kee could only stare at him in surprise. Four months ago he'd been pissed as hell that Tim, his best friend who he'd flown with for a decade, had been bumped over to Henderson's helo to make room for her. She'd also been a baby Night Stalker fresh out of training.

She now had a place aboard a DAP Hawk, the respect of her teammates, and Archie and Dilya waiting for her. Didn't mean there wasn't more to prove…

But John nodded that he meant it. Wild!

Dusty fended off Tim with enough force to flip his chair over, with Tim still in it.

Kee and Big John lifted their trays off the table just in time; in Tim's backward flail, he kicked the bottom of the table. Curses sounded all down the length of it as glasses and sodas toppled.

The two of them set their trays back down.

"Uh, thanks," was all she could think to say.

"Nothing but the truth," John nodded as he returned to eating.

"What's the truth?" Tim righted his chair and thumped his butt back into it.

"That you aren't worth the trouble of even knowing, shithead," John rumbled out.

"Hey, somebody's got to keep things lively," then, as if nothing had happened, Tim grinned and continued eating Kee's slice of garlic bread that had started the whole hoopla.

CHAPTER 4

"It will be okay," though Archie wasn't sure which of them he was reassuring. He and Dilya stood on the tarmac outside Hangar Four on the military side of Pisa's Galileo Galilei Airport. She held his hand tightly.

It had been two months since they'd seen Kee in person. She'd managed a few video calls, but Dilya didn't seem to understand those. What if they'd grown distant?

Dilya had built her sand sculpture around some image of Kee the mother figure. Kee was many things, but that wasn't one of them. She was tender with Dilya, but he wouldn't describe her as maternal.

Tugging his hand, Dilya pointed suddenly at the sky.

Archie squinted up at the plane and waited for it to resolve from being a tiny black dot coming toward the runway. Four-engine turboprop. Hercules C-130. He squeezed her hand, hoping that this was it.

Dilya squared her shoulders and checked her clothes. She had adopted portions of American teen style, but made it her own. Her Muslim heritage had stuck in her modesty, and he could only hope that lasted. Leggings under khaki shorts. A loose blouse that hid her pre-teen curves and a stone-washed denim jacket despite the September warmth. A trio of light scarves braided into a multi-colored neon twist meant this was her fancy wear for special occasions—at least that's how he was interpreting it.

He'd put on tan khakis and a black t-shirt without thinking about it—standard off-duty wear. Except he was *way* off duty.

There was a bright screech of tires as the plane touched down, followed immediately by the heavy roar of the four eight-bladed propellers reversing hard to dump speed. His nerves were climbing irrationally but he couldn't stop them.

"I'd rather be facing a ZU-23," a particularly lethal Russian-made anti-aircraft gun.

Dilya looked up at him strangely.

"Never mind." Some things were unexplainable, even if she was getting the language. He concentrated on keeping his grasp on her hand light and calm.

The big plane rolled up, shut down, then lowered its rear ramp.

"Hey, Arch!" Big John strode down the ramp and came over to lock him in a bear hug while Tim thumped him hard on the back. Major Henderson strolled up and shook his hand hard enough that Archie could only hope that the doctors had reattached his shoulder as solidly as they said they had.

Emily walked up to him. Ten years they'd flown together. Ever since she'd picked him out of the crowd at West Point in a History of the Military Art course, they'd served side by side. She was so far out of his league, that there had never been anything between them. Or maybe the spark had simply never been there in the first place.

She reached out and rested her hand as lightly as a feather on his shoulder before looking directly at him.

He nodded. Yes, it was all okay, even if he could never fly beside her again.

Emily squeezed his shoulder lightly in acknowledgement. Between them there was no need for words.

Then, unexpectedly, she shifted her hand to his cheek and offered him a nod. "It's all good, Archie."

He tried to see what she meant, but couldn't read the expression on her face. Finally, Emily offered one of her fleeting, all-knowing smiles. Then she nodded behind herself, where she couldn't possibly see what was happening.

There, kneeling at the foot of the ramp, was the most amazing woman he'd ever met. Her arms were filled with Dilya who had a throttle-hold around Kee's neck.

But even as her hands were reassuring the little girl, her dark eyes were watching him.

Archie didn't even remember walking away from Emily and crossing to her. It was a short distance, one measured in barely noticed handshakes and hearty congratulations.

Two months since he'd seen her and Kee looked even more incredible than he'd remembered. Barely five-six, powerful curves, soldier strong, dark brown hair that fell straight to her jawline, and her trademark thin strip of golden blond. Her dark past was always with her.

She rose to her feet, holding Dilya lightly in her arms.

She didn't open one arm to greet him in—it wasn't her way. Didn't even smile which was a little odd.

But when he wrapped his arms around both of them, she did bury her face against his new shoulder and breathe him in.

He kissed them both on top of the head and then prayed that he wouldn't screw this up.

CHAPTER 5

"What do you think?" Kee did a little dance in front of the mirror. At the moment, she, Dilya, Emily, and Archie's mom, Betty, had command of the little wedding dress shop. Outside the window, Italy was bustling by and she couldn't wait to get out into the sunshine and play.

The dress landed dangerously high on the thigh—no sitting down in this one. The cleavage had been designed with someone like her in mind. Wedding lace of the purest white made her tan-dark skin stand out and the racing-strip red trim just screamed wild and sexy.

"This will just kill Archie. I know it will."

A quick spin as she watched in the mirror convinced her of its awesomeness for liquifying men's brains on first sight.

"Seriously, could it be any better?" She spun once more and stopped facing Dilya.

Dilya sat in the pink-and-white armchair with her head down on the knees she was pulling tight against her chest. The other arm was over the top of her head as if to make sure she didn't accidentally look up.

"C'mon, kid. A little skin isn't going to burn out your eyes."

"What means burn out—" Dilya started to look up, saw Kee, yelped, and ducked her head back down.

Kee looked at the ceiling and sighed. "This isn't happening."

She looked helplessly over at the shop clerk who merely shrugged. Wedding dresses weren't a big stock item at a forward operating base in a dark corner of northern Pakistan, so she'd had to wait for Italy to buy one.

Archie and the boys had been shooed off to Vernazza (about an hour train ride up the coast) for a bachelor's party —or at least to visit a good *taverna*. Vernazza had been one of their favorite towns when they visited here before the fateful mission that had wounded Archie. It also had a harbor deep enough for the sailboat they'd be honeymooning on so that they could leave directly from the ceremony.

He'd looked an absolute wreck—a gorgeous one, but a wreck. His wavy brown hair had been lightened by the sun and his tan had been darkened, making him even more impossibly handsome. But it was his eyes that had gotten to her. She'd felt consumed by his wide, sky-blue eyes.

All through lunch he hadn't stopped staring at her, and wouldn't let go of her hand. He was being a little intense for her and it was kind of freaking her out. On the other hand, she'd missed him the moment he'd left for the train. Kee did her best to ignore that fact because it didn't sound at all like her.

Meanwhile, the women had stayed in Pisa to do a little shopping, especially dress shopping.

"Oh my," Betty looked Kee up and down as she came out of the racks, carrying a pretty Italian sundress covered with stylized sweet pea blossoms that would look great on such an elegant woman. "Well, that will surely get Archie's attention.

Although, I'm not sure if he'll be able to say his vows if you are wearing that."

"That's what I like about it."

Emily peeked over the barrier of one of the changing rooms. Kee could see the smile reach Emily's eyes, though she didn't say a word.

"Dilya doesn't approve."

The girl just squeaked, but didn't raise her head.

"She may have a point," Emily stepped through the swinging door that had masked her from eyes to knees. She looked amazing. Her slender form was perfectly outlined in a clinging sheath dress that was the same light topaz blue as her eyes.

"Well, if I had a figure like yours, I'd steal that dress right off your back. How is someone who looks like me supposed to look that beautiful? Skin is reliable—works every time."

Emily, Betty, and the shop clerk began running her through different dresses. Kee didn't let them take away the hot little number, though they tried several times.

By dress six—or maybe it was sixteen—her patience was wearing thin. Didn't Italian women have breasts? They must all be as slender as the major or as elegant as Archie's mom. The wedding dresses that were built for women with a full figure assumed they were far taller than she was. Or didn't have hips to match. Or had the breasts and hips, but also the waist to go with them.

There was no time for alterations. Most of the team was on a three-day pass: a day to get here, the ceremony tomorrow, and a day to get back. She was pretty touched at how many of them had come. The only one missing was—

"Hey, where's Connie? Did anyone think to invite her?"

Emily nodded. "She didn't want to intrude."

Huh! Not the cold bitch that Kee had first assumed—nor the chill soldier either. Hadn't guessed at her being sensitive.

Being shy wasn't something Kee had a lot of experience with, but that would explain a lot. Made her actually like the woman. Definitely had to check her out more after the honeymoon.

"Well, I'm pretty much sunk here. Dilya will just have to suck it up and—"

But when she turned for the changing room, a dress hung on the door. It was really pretty, with a high neck, half sleeves, and a long skirt made of a few overlapping layers of lace beneath a sheer.

Emily stepped up beside her and after a long moment's inspection made a considering "Hmmm" sound. Betty and the shop clerk were still rummaging through the racks.

Dilya was back in her armchair watching Kee intently.

A cheer roared through the sports bar as a television showed the Italian soccer team scoring, then heartrending groans as a ref signaled a disallowed goal, made the sign for pushing, and tossed the ball to the French goalie to bring it back into play.

Archie leaned against the wall behind his chair. They'd shoved him into the back of the corner table then sandwiched him in to either side. Major Henderson, Big John, Tim, Dusty, Captain Richardson, and some of the Little Bird pilots as well.

Perhaps they were being friendly. Or perhaps they understood just how close he was to hitting the ground running and not stopping until he hit Kansas.

He let the conversation drift back and forth, mostly without him, only dipping into the air turbulence of the talk when he couldn't avoid it.

Somehow they'd found a sports bar in Italy that was both Italian and so very not. Big screen TVs were mounted all around a room that had been built of stone around the time of Charlemagne, or maybe Caesar. But rather than the

American fare of baseball, football, and boxing, they were serving out soccer, Formula 1 auto racing, and cricket. The bar was lined with taps that read: Peroni, Heineken Italia, Menabrea, Tarricone, and other beers he'd never heard of. There was a domed, wood-fired pizza oven, covered in black-and-white tiles patterned like a soccer ball.

There were other differences from American bars as well. Far more couples than single men, and kids too. And as often as not when there was a baby or toddler, it was the father tending to it rather than the mom. There was a lively, happy buzz, all of it in flowing Italian that sounded almost as beautiful as Spanish.

"Scares you spitless, doesn't it?" Mark boomed out cheerfully from one side. To his other side, Big John had a liter glass wrapped in one of his big hands. Tim had dragged the others up to the bar where he was calling play by play on a rugby game that he clearly didn't understand. The Italians at the bar were joining in the spirit of it and misdirecting him at every chance.

Archie weighed the odds of getting past Mark or Big John and decided that his chances were too slim.

Unable to speak, he could only nod.

Mark answered his nod sagely, still wearing his mirrored shades despite the bar's dim interior. "Know the feeling. The day I stood at the head of that aisle with Emily walking toward me? That's the day they should have awarded me the Medal of Honor for bravery far exceeding the call of duty."

"Don't sound so scary to me," Big John knocked back a large swallow of beer.

"Just wait until it's your turn," Mark scoffed. "How about that cute new girl on your team? What's her name? Connie something?"

John flinched badly enough to shake the table.

Archie didn't know who they were talking about. It felt

strange to not know something about the company. As if he belonged even less than he'd thought he did, which wasn't much any more.

"Not a chance. That woman is enough to drive a dude batshit."

"Willing to bet a twenty on that?" Mark slapped a twenty-euro note on the table.

"No way, asshole," John was shaking his head. "Makes me ill just thinking about it."

"That's Major Asshole to you," Mark tried pushing his twenty across, but John wasn't taking it.

"No argument from me on that one, boss." John glared down at his beer.

Archie was fine with the conversation moving on without him. Maybe he could just fade away. Dilya seemed to do that sometimes, just suddenly—not be there. It was scary as hell when she did it unexpectedly. She'd even managed to slip aboard a black ops mission with them once with no one the wiser until it was too late to turn back. Turned out in the end that it was a good thing she had.

"You know..." John cricked his neck. "Don't know if I should be saying this, but your bride is kinda wound up about this as well."

"Kee?" Archie shook his head. "No, John. You're reading that wrong. Kee always has her act together. Knows exactly what she wants."

"Willing to bet a twenty on that?" Mark tried shoving the bill in his direction.

"Don't, Archie," Big John warned. "That's a sure loss. Chick is freakin'."

"But if she doesn't want to marry me then..." Archie tapered off as John seemed to grow twice his already substantial size.

"I didn't say that. Just said she was freaking. Time to man

up, dude. You don't put a ring on that gal's finger tomorrow, you aren't gonna be nothing but a bloody smear on the sidewalk. Don't care what your rank is, sir. This is man to man."

Archie studied his beer. It sounded as if Kee wanted out.

Or maybe not. She was here in Italy and out buying a dress. By nightfall, they'd be in the same hotel room. All through lunch he'd kept looking at her in surprise, trying to figure out how he could be lucky enough to marry her.

And there was no questioning the way that she'd held Dilya when she stepped off the plane.

And no questioning the way she'd let him hold the two of them. Just as Dilya had carved it in the sand. And when he'd seen the photo, he remembered how he'd felt, as if his heart couldn't get any fuller.

Time to man up, dude. Good advice.

"Still a got a twenty on you and Connie, John," Mark's expression was inscrutable behind his mirrored shades. "What do you say? Want some easy money?"

Big John snarled, hauled out his wallet and slapped a pair of twenties on the table. "I'll take that bet twice. Double no-way no-how."

Henderson nodded happily and refreshed all of their glasses from the pitcher.

CHAPTER 7

Kee lay awake on the big bed.

Vernazza wasn't that big a town. A small harbor, mostly filled with fishing skiffs behind a long breakwater. Behind the seawall, it was really just a single circle street with a lot of small branches to the sides. Tucked up against the cliffs of Liguria, it was one of the five towns that made up Cinque Terre.

So after arriving on the train and leaving their new dresses at the hotel, they had gone out for their own small gal celebration. Gelato then a sausage and pepper calzone—in that order. Pear gelato was in season and it wasn't worth missing it. She and Dilya had split a second one after dinner, though Emily and Betty had declared one was sufficient.

They'd seen the bar where the men had ended up—it wasn't hard to find as it had the rowdiest crowd anywhere in the tiny town. They'd stood outside in the falling darkness and looked in through the window. Archie and Tim facing off against a pair of Italian men at a foosball table with a big crowd gathered around them. Archie looked a little manic—

cheering his own team, gasping in despair at each loss, and crowing with each victory.

It wasn't like him, and Kee still lay awake contemplating the meaning of it all.

Dilya, originally set to sleep on the couch in their room, had slipped into bed with her and Kee had let her. Her nerves were calmer when the girl was with her. Everything somehow made sense—which was ridiculous, because Kee was supposed to be dead.

She'd never expected to live this long—nearly hadn't twice and she had the scars to prove it. Yet against all odds, she had. Not just survived, but tomorrow would become both wife and adoptive mother. That wasn't on any life plan she'd ever had.

The door opened quietly.

Kee narrowed her eyes so that they wouldn't catch the nightlight she'd left on.

Archie peeked in. Not the wild man she'd barely recognized at the foosball table. Instead, it was the man she'd known from the first day. He stood just inside the door: shoes in his hand, silent, watching.

Considerate, thoughtful. That was Archie.

But he kept standing there. Looking down at her and Dilya as a smile slowly grew on his face. He'd looked so serious at the airport, which had completely unnerved her. But now—even in the dim light—she could see the lopsided smile that she so loved settle over him. That was the man she was marrying.

He watched them for a few moments before going over to the couch. It wasn't near long enough for a grown man, it was barely long enough for Dilya. But he didn't seem to mind. Instead, he simply curled up with that goofy smile on his face.

She fell asleep with him watching over his new family.

CHAPTER 8

*A*rchie wasn't sure if he'd eaten dinner, but he'd surely drunk it. Attempting to sleep off the aftereffects—while twisted up like a pretzel on the short couch—hadn't worked.

Mark handed him several aspirin and a double espresso, then dug out his uniform and began ironing it for him. If there was one thing the Army taught you, it was how to have an immaculate uniform.

Kee and Dilya were gone of course.

He showered, dressed, and was fed more coffee before he truly regained consciousness. He came to stand at the altar.

"Hell of a setting you chose," Mark sounded pleased.

Archie could only squint against the brightness of the morning. They stood at the end of the tiny harbor's massive breakwater. To his back was a line of huge stones that were piled a story tall above the quiet Mediterranean. It was hard to believe that it served a purpose, yet he'd seen pictures of the winter storms blowing fifty feet of spray up against its stout bulwark.

In front of him Vernazza harbor stretched only a few

hundred feet from side to side. In the middle floated the thirty-foot sloop he'd rented in La Spezia and brought here two days ago. That was his honeymoon with Kee—sailing along the Ligurian and Amalfi coast while Dilya was off with his parents.

Instead of romantic, it now sounded sad. Part of their courtship had been aboard a sailboat, poking their way down this very coast. But picturing someone as vital as Kee with a husband as directionless as himself…not a good image.

Vernazza itself filled the cul-de-sac formed by the sea cliffs with four- and five-story buildings clustered so tightly together that it was hard to imagine there were cobbled streets winding among them—deep in shadow and spangled with surprising patches of sunlight. The buildings were the red and oranges of sunset, accented by the lone white bell tower of the Santa Margherita church. He could just make out the clock that said ten minutes to ten o'clock. Beyond the town, a steeply terraced vineyard masked any harsh stone with a bounty of grape vines.

At the far end of the breakwater, guarding the original entrance to the harbor against pirates before the breakwater had been built, Doria Castle commanded the town. It perched atop a high rocky bluff.

Vernazza was ancient. Solid. It dated back a thousand years and might be much unchanged for another thousand.

It made Archie feel unimportant, even ephemeral.

"I have no place here." He knew it. No place to serve. He was about to marry a woman he could no longer serve beside. What was he doing? It wasn't right. He should—

"Been meaning to talk to you about that," Mark was looking at him.

Archie could only look at the twin pretender version of himself reflected back at him by the major's sunglasses. Even the uniform felt wrong. Archie had flown beside Emily for a decade since West Point and now he wore the dress uniform as if he somehow still belonged.

"You're back on the active duty?"

"Light duty," Archie grunted out. "They said it will be a year before I can fly again. You know as well as I do what that does to a flier's skills." It would take another year after that to get his skills back up to Night Stalker standards, if he even could.

Mark turned to track a pair of stunning brunettes in European-skimpy bikinis as they headed out to lie on the rocks and do a little sunbathing. They, in turn, definitely had eyes for the two men in full American military dress uniforms.

Archie was too tired to do more than notice them, despite their coy looks and increased hip sway.

"Been missing you in operations," Mark said without facing him.

"Great." He must be recovering from last night's excesses —definitely his most excessive ever—because he'd managed to rediscover sarcasm.

"Emily is the queen of tactical, but we never understood just how much you brought to the game strategically. You see the big picture far faster than anyone else in the entire company. If you hadn't been so powerful a team—the strategic and the tactical together—you'd have had your own bird a long time ago."

"Never cared about that. Not gonna happen now anyway, is it?" Archie tried to shake off being so morose. It was a more unfamiliar coat that the dress uniform he now wore. But the doubt still stuck to his shoulders.

Archie glanced at Mark, but he was walking away to greet the Army Chaplin who had taken the train up from Camp Darby in Pisa. Probably hadn't even heard Archie's complaint.

Others began arriving. Tim and Big John weren't in formal blue mess dress uniforms, but were definitely cutting a swath in their Army service uniforms. Their passage along the breakwater had collected a small gaggle of tourist admirers, and a few locals as well. They each had an Italian beauty on their arm—ones Archie vaguely recalled from the bar last night.

There wasn't room for chairs or aisles, but there were two rises in the concrete backing for the breakwater that were soon filled as benches. He'd been thrilled that Mark and some of the other guys had come. He was an only child and Kee had no family at all, so it was nice to have the extra people. But as more gawkers drifted their way, it became clear that they were going to have a big wedding after all.

Big John came up and slapped his back with enough cheerful bonhomie to drive the last of Archie's hangover into the Vernazza harbor.

"Looking awesome, sir," Tim saluted him.

"Feeling like shit, Tim," Archie returned the gesture.

"No way," Big John grabbed him by the shoulder and shook him in a friendly fashion that almost took Archie's feet out from under him. "You can't be—not with what you're about to do. Remember what I said last night."

Archie looked down at the storm-weathered concrete and wondered if Big John really would deliver on his threat to squish him into it if he was dumb enough to not marry Kee. So, he changed the subject.

"I'm never, ever going drinking with you two again. And that's an order."

"Yes, sir!" Big John saluted this time.

"Sounds like a bet," Tim looked ready to rush off and find a six-pack in order to take up the challenge right then and there.

Archie went for another subject change, "Like the bet John made that he wasn't going to fall for Connie."

"Connie?" Tim turned on his friend utterly delighted. "You and the egghead mechanic? Dude, I didn't know. When's the wedding?"

"The twelfth of never," Big John grumbled.

"No, seriously. She's cute as hell. Weird in several ways, but majorly cute."

"Fine, you can have her," John was all magnanimity.

"Not if you already got a bet on."

"He bet me," Mark rejoined them, "that he *wasn't* going to fall for her."

"Oh!" Tim crowed. "This is gonna be so excellent!"

Tim and Big John began arguing about it in the way only best friends could.

The crowd was thickening. Soon, the entire breakwater would be crammed full.

Archie needed to talk to Kee, try to talk her out of it, before it was too late. But there was no way that he was going to get to talk to her before the ceremony.

The church tower clock read five minutes to ten. Five minutes to their agreed start time.

Could he do it at the altar?

Should he?

This couldn't be happening.

CHAPTER 9

"There's no way I can do this!" Kee looked down at the waterfront aghast.

A small cluster of men in full military uniforms stood at the end of the breakwater. Even at this distance, Archie and Mark stood out in their dress uniforms with wide red lapels, white shirt fronts, and blue pants with gold stripes on the side. Between her and the wedding party were hundreds of tourists. Everything from sundresses to jeans with bikini tops. Men, women, teens, baby strollers, octogenarians: an entire slice of Italian locals and tourists.

Emily offered one of her all-knowing smiles while Betty patted her arm consolingly.

Dilya clung to her hand.

The four of them had enjoyed a quiet breakfast of lattes and cornetto pastries, with Dilya drinking a cup of hot chocolate almost as big as her head.

"We'll just forge a path for you," Emily went to step out of the hotel entry overlooking the harbor. Kee grabbed her and pulled her back.

"It's not the people that are freaking me out."

Emily furrowed her brow at Kee. Betty was also looking confused.

"Look. For both of you marriage was a logical step."

"So not," Emily started. "I never—"

"But you did," Kee cut her off. "Your parents were married. Had a kid. Raised you. All of that. It's natural to you."

Kee managed to drag in a breath, but any calm that she needed just wasn't climbing aboard.

"I'm being serious here, I was born on the streets. Mom took care of me when she wasn't too stoned to remember who I was. Marriage was something the judge did for people who somehow thought they'd last more than a year or two together. I sure never did. I *can't* be someone's wife. I *can't* be someone's mother." She looked down at Dilya who was watching the whole tirade with worry, but probably didn't understand one word in ten.

Kee held up their joined hands to demonstrate. "This isn't me!"

For once Emily didn't have some simple answer. And that was even more scary, because Emily knew everything.

"I love Archie. I'm sure of that. But being a Wife and Mother, how am I supposed to do that? I don't even know what that means or what it's supposed to look like. I—"

Betty rested a hand on Kee's arm which felt as if it was all she that kept her from flying apart. "I wasn't a good mother."

"But," Kee waved her hand helplessly toward the waterfront, "Archie. He's such an amazing man. You did that."

Betty tipped her head for a moment. "You were the one who pointed that out to me, not many miles from here— back when we first met and I didn't know or trust you. I still find it to be a curious thought. Yes, I love my son and he *has* become an amazing man, *despite* my feeble attempts at bringing him up properly. I have given this a great deal of thought since then."

"Please tell me you learned something?" Kee peeked out the window at the still-growing crowd and shivered.

"I learned—"

Dilya tugged on Kee's arm, pulling until she had to kneel to face her.

"What?"

Dilya brushed her hands over Kee's hair, then her neck and shoulders as if trying to tell her something. Then, after a sigh, reached into a pocket of her dress and pulled out two squares of tightly folded cloth.

Kee recognized them right away. It was the two scarves they had bought together in a Pakastani market a lifetime ago. Kee had forgotten about them, but apparently Dilya hadn't.

She very carefully unfolded Kee's scarf. The edge trim of the green of new life surrounded a field of midnight blue filled with stars—a masterpiece of weaving craft. It had been her Night Stalker scarf.

Dilya folded it point to point then rolled it like a bandana. It wouldn't go with her hair and around her neck it would break the line of the wedding dress. But Kee decided it was best to keep her thoughts to herself.

She needn't have worried. Dilya wrapped it several times around Kee's wrist and tied the ends together making a Night Stalker bracelet of the beautiful cloth.

Kee took Dilya's far simpler scarf, a field of the same green with the dark blue for trim, and tied it over Dilya's hair as would be appropriately modest for her Muslim heritage. She took a moment to finger brush Dilya's thick hair back over her shoulders.

Then Dilya hugged her. Not the fierce hug of greeting at the airport that had almost choked out tears along with Kee's breath. Instead, it was simply a hug of childish love. Except there had never been anything childish about Dilya. Nothing in her hard past had allowed for something as simple as childhood. It was but one of the true bonds between them.

"That is what I learned," Betsy whispered quietly. "I can't picture myself being a good mother or a good wife. But I *can* picture a good mother or wife being me. Something in who I am made Archie. Not what I think I should have been, just in who I was. And who I am with his father, my husband. You will be an amazing mother and wife, Kee, because it is already in you."

Kee took Dilya's hand again as she rose back to her feet.

Emily wasn't looking at her, but rather down at Dilya in surprise. With a look that Kee now understood. For the first time, the daunting Major Emily Beale was also realizing that she could be a mother someday—without changing the magnificent woman she was.

"Magnificent woman," Kee said it softly. "Magnificent *women*," she declared with more certainty. "The four of us are magnificent, aren't we?"

Betty and then Emily nodded tentatively once. Then again with growing smiles.

"Let's do this."

And Dilya held her hand tightly as they stepped out of the hotel entry and onto the crowded street.

CHAPTER 10

Archie looked up as the church bell began striking ten o'clock. It echoed across the harbor and town so clearly that speech became difficult.

Then he spotted the women the instant they stepped out of the hotel door, though they were on the far side of the harbor.

"You ready, Archie?" Mark shouted above the bell as it switched from ringing the hour to playing some involved piece of music. He clamped a hand on Archie's shoulder as if to make sure he didn't simply dive into the harbor and swim for the sailboat...or maybe just straight out to sea.

"No!"

Mark started to laugh, but cut it off after he looked at Archie's face.

"So help me to god, Mark. How am I supposed to saddle Kee with a husband who can't even be with her? Who can no longer serve?" He flapped his arm and ignored the deep pinch. *Who isn't even a whole man?* "Being a pilot is all I ever was. And now I'm not even that."

"You wait until the bride is walking toward you to tell me

this shit?" Mark actually shoved his sunglasses up into his hair revealing his steel-gray eyes. He squinted for a long moment. "No… Tell me you aren't about to do something as stupid as I think you are."

Archie could only shrug and watch the four women as they reached the waterfront and began circling around the harbor. Emily in blue, Mom in a pretty sundress, and two women wrapped in the lightest shade of gold, lit by the morning sun until they shone.

Others in the crowd began noticing the approaching processional and quieted until the only sound was the bright ringing of the church bells. A narrow aisle was slowly forming through the heart of the crowd as people pressed aside.

"Archie, you're an idiot," Mark's whisper sounded fierce.

"Wouldn't surprise me," Archie kept watching Kee's approach and wondered how he should do it. Take her aside before the ceremony could start? And Dilya. How was he supposed to tell Dilya?

Mark snarled and grabbed his shoulder, forcing him to turn away. When he saw Mark's expression, Archie almost stepped backward off the breakwater and into the waves lapping directly below. Mark didn't look angry, he looked furious. His gray eyes had darkened until Archie wondered if he was about to be killed.

"Don't you *dare* do that to these women! That's a direct order, Captain Stevenson."

Archie kept his thoughts about civilian versus military spheres of control to himself.

"Shit!" Mark glanced up the breakwater where Kee and Dilya had disappeared into the back of the crowd.

Only the shining blonde of Emily's hair was high enough to show their progress through the gathered masses.

"I've got about thirty seconds, so just shut up and listen."

Archie shrugged his acquiescence. Nothing was going to change his mind, no matter how much it was hurting his heart. It was going to hurt Kee and Dilya, and it was going to kill him. But it was his job to protect them, even if it was from himself.

"I told you we've been feeling the pinch of not having you as the team's strategist."

"So?"

"Told you to shut up. I was going to tell you after your honeymoon. I structured the 5th Battalion D Company without an AMC. I didn't want some backfield, Air Mission Commander messing with my team—especially not some asshole who wasn't good enough to *fly* with my team. I built this company from the ground up and it only gets the best. That includes you, asshole. You're back in forward operations as fast as I can get you there. But you'll be flying in a command helo, well behind the line of fire, where you can direct the whole team."

Archie could only blink as his world shifted.

"You screw this up and Big John won't have a chance to pummel you because I'll beat the shit out of you myself. Do you understand me, soldier?"

Archie did. Not entirely, but enough that he managed a slow nod.

"You say one word other than 'I do' before this is over and I'll go from being your best man to your worst nightmare. You got that?"

"...I do," Archie managed.

Mark barked out a laugh, then slapped him hard on his bad shoulder.

Archie didn't flinch. It didn't hurt as much as he'd have expected.

He turned to face the approaching wedding party.

His mom and Emily led the way.

Dilya came next, in a modest dress, with leggings beneath and her favorite scarf covering her hair. There was the child of his heart. Someday he and Kee might have a child of their own, but it would be impossible to love it more than the war orphan that they'd be adopting as part of the wedding ceremony. The Chaplin had all of the official forms already prepared.

And then he saw Kee. Saw her and understood so much that hadn't been clear to him even moments ago.

She wore a dress of lightest gold that transformed her from the impossibly beautiful soldier to a glorious bride. It rode high up her neck, emphasizing the amazing line of her neck and strong shoulders. It hugged her generous curves proving that while she might be a warrior, she was also the embodiment of pure womanhood. A high slit in the long skirt revealed the occasional flash of her amazing legs, accenting Kee's inherent sexiness.

But there were two things that confirmed for him that he'd never have turned from her at this altar, even without Mark's surprising offer to rejoin the company.

On her wrist Kee wore the scarf that she and Dilya had purchased together. A connection so deep between the woman and girl. They were already family and it was breathtaking that they were letting him in.

The second was the color of the dress. It exactly matched the thin strip of Kee's dark hair that she always kept dyed bright blonde in memory of a friend who had been the one light in her ever-so-dark past. But now it was transformed. That tiny anomaly would now always represent her wedding dress and this day as well. It was absolutely transformative. How could he not love a woman who could pass through the trials she had and still let him all the way into her heart?

He broke Mark's mandate as she came to stand beside

him before the Chaplin and whispered four words softly enough to be for her ears only.

"Night Stalkers Don't Quit."

She mouthed them back.

And looked at him with a third reason his next words would be "I do."

Just as on that first day, she looked at him with those beautiful dark eyes that showed all of her heart so clearly. That showed that she too would have sacrificed everything to protect their family.

Not because that was what a Night Stalker would do.

Because that is what a family did when the love was as true as theirs.

FRANK'S INDEPENDENCE DAY (EXCERPT)

IF YOU LIKED KEE, YOU'LL LOVE BEAT

Frank Adams had his boys slide up around the metallic-blue late-model BMW at the stop light on Amsterdam Ave. One stood by the passenger door, one ahead, one behind, and he took the driver's window himself as usual.

It was only the third time they'd done this, but Frank saw, without really watching, that they made it look smooth. They'd split the thousand that the chop shop had just paid for the Ford they'd jacked and two grand for the Camry. But a new Beemer? That was a serious score. What they were doing so far uptown this late on a hot, New York night was the driver's own damn fault.

He started it like any standard windshield scam. Spray the windshield to blind the driver, then shake them down for five bucks to clean it so they can see to drive away. The bright bite of ammonia almost reassuring to New Yorkers who had come to expect the scam. He'd long since learned to flick the windshield wiper up so that the driver couldn't just clean their own damn window. It was when the driver's window rolled down, and the person at the wheel started griping, that the real action would begin.

A glance to the sides showed not much traffic. Lot of folks gone down by the water to watch the fireworks, or off with family for July 4th picnics at the park, or on their fire escapes in the sweltering summer heat. The acrid sting of burnt cordite hung like a haze over the city from a million firecrackers, bottle rockets, M-80s, cherry bombs, and everything else legal or not. Hell, Chinatown would be sounding like they were tossing around sticks of dynamite.

Night had settled on the roads out of Columbia University and into his end of Manhattan, and as much darkness as could ever be happening beneath the New York City lights had done gone and happened.

Frank's boys were doing good. At the front and back, they'd leaned casually on the hood and trunk of the car not facing the prize, but instead watching lookout up and down the length of Amsterdam Ave. They'd shout if any cops surfaced.

And no self-respecting BMW driver would run over someone they didn't know just to get away, especially ones who weren't even looking at them threateningly.

Other drivers were accelerating sharply and running the red light just so they weren't a part of whatever was going down at the corner of Amsterdam and midnight.

Three minutes. That meant they had about three minutes until someone nerved down enough to find a pay phone and call the cops and he and his boys had to be gone.

They'd only need about one.

The Beemer jerked back about two feet with little more than a hiss and a throb from that smooth, cool engine.

His boys were on the pavement before Frank could even blink.

Japs had been sitting on the trunk but was now

sprawled on his face and Hale sat abruptly on his butt when the car's hood pulled out from underneath him. It was almost funny, the two of them looked so damn surprised.

Then he was facing the rolled down window, just as he'd planned. He could taste the new-car fine-leather smell as it wafted out.

What he hadn't planned was to be staring right down the barrel of a .357. Abruptly, all he could taste was the metal sting of adrenaline and the stink of his own sweat.

He'd seen enough guns to know that the Smith & Wesson 66 was not some normal bad-ass revolver.

He was facing death right between the eyes.

His body froze so hard he didn't even drop the knife nestled out of sight in his palm.

The woman who looked at him, right hand aiming the gun across her body, left hand still on the wheel, had the blackest eyes he'd ever seen. So dark that no light came back from them, like looking down twin barrels of death even more dangerous than the gun's.

A cop siren sounded in the distance, but his boys were already on the move out of there.

"They're leaving you behind."

Her voice was as smooth as her weapon. Calm, not all nervy like someone surprised by a carjacking or unfamiliar with the weapon she held rock steady.

"What I told 'em to do."

"Don't risk the whole team?"

He shrugged a yes.

That siren was getting louder and it was starting to worry him. But even doing a drop and run, well... He was fast, but not faster than a .357. He stayed put. Classy lady in a Beemer and a dead carjacker, she wasn't risking any real trouble if she gunned him down where he stood.

"Decision point. Go down for it. Spend some time in juvie—"

"I'm twenty, twenty-one next week." Why'd he been dumb enough to say that? Not that the cops wouldn't find out, but they didn't have his prints anywhere in their system… yet. He didn't carry any ID either, but there was only so long you could play that card.

"Okay, do some time or get in the car."

He looked into the deep well of those dark eyes, allowing himself three heartbeats to decide what the hell she was up to. The sharp squeal of cop tires swerving around some other car too few blocks away won the argument.

Frank moved around the front of the car fast, flicking down the wiper blade as he went, and slid into her passenger seat.

While he circled, she'd shifted the big gun into her left hand. Could shoot with either hand, that took training. Some off duty cop in a Beemer, just his luck.

He was barely in the car when the fuzz rounded the corner, their lights going.

"Buckle up."

It was only after he buckled in that another thought struck him. A bad one. She just might drive him somewhere, gun him down, and dump his body. Never knew with cops in this town. Then she wouldn't even have to fill out any damn paperwork. *Little bit late to think of that shit, Adams. Dumbass!* Once around the passenger side, he should have just kept running, not climbed into the lady's damn car like a whatever it was that went to the slaughter. Sheep? Calves? Something. Frank Adamses.

She slid the gun under the flap of her leather vest so that it was out of sight, but still aimed at him across her body. She ran the windshield wiper and together they watched the blue-and-white roll up fast. The cops pulled up driver to driver, facing the wrong way on the street to do so.

"Everything okay, ma'am?"

Frank had the distinct impression that even though the woman was reassuring the cop, if Frank so much as flinched, there'd be a big, bad hole in his chest and that the thing that would really tick her off was the damage to her German-engineered car door where the bullet would punch a good-sized hole after making a real mess of his body on its way through. It took her long enough to talk the cop down that Frank had time to register how the car's seat fit to his body. It was way more comfortable than any chair or sofa he'd ever slouched in. Damn seat alone probably cost more than everything he owned.

Finally satisfied, only after blinding Frank with a big flashlight a couple of times, the cops rolled away real slow. He'd purposely dressed okay in his best jeans and a loose button-down shirt he'd worn to Levon's courtroom wedding. That way he wasn't too scary for the windshield-washing scam to work. It paid off now, he didn't look too out of place in this classy car. He eyed the woman carefully, as classy looking as her vehicle. Or even more.

She pulled her hand out from under her vest of dark leather even finer than the seat upholstery, leaving the gun behind, and rolled up the window. Shoulder holster. He'd tried to carjack a woman who wore a .357 in a shoulder holster. What were the chances of that kind of bad luck? Well, one in three. Third carjacking ever, woman with large gun. Not exactly high-level math.

Though he'd never heard of anything like it on the street. He'd been told to watch for crazies, diving for glove compartments and purses, so full of nerves that they were more danger to themselves than anyone else. Best advice on those had been to run. Toward the back of the car. Make yourself a hard shot when they're all buckled in and facing forward. They'd be undertrained, have lousy aim, and probably wouldn't shoot if they thought they'd won. That's if they could find the damn safety.

Not this lady. Cool and calm.

He'd bet she could execute his ass without havin' a bad night's sleep.

"Let's go somewhere and talk." With the window up, the air-con dropped the temperature about twenty degrees from the July heat blast going on out in the real world which was sweet, but left a chill up his spine that started right where his butt was planted in the fine leather seat.

She punched the gas and popped the clutch, in seconds they were hurtling downtown on Amsterdam and Frank knew he better hang on for dear life.

Available at fine retailers everywhere.
Frank's Independence Day

ABOUT THE AUTHOR

M.L. Buchman started the first of, what is now over 50 novels and as many short stories, while flying from South Korea to ride his bicycle across the Australian Outback. Part of a solo around the world trip that ultimately launched his writing career.

All three of his military romantic suspense series—The Night Stalkers, Firehawks, and Delta Force—have had a title named "Top 10 Romance of the Year" by the American Library Association's *Booklist*. NPR and Barnes & Noble have named other titles "Top 5 Romance of the Year." In 2016 he was a finalist for Romance Writers of America prestigious RITA award. He also writes: contemporary romance, thrillers, and fantasy.

Past lives include: years as a project manager, rebuilding and single-handing a fifty-foot sailboat, both flying and jumping out of airplanes, and he has designed and built two houses. He is now making his living as a full-time writer on the Oregon Coast with his beloved wife and is constantly amazed at what you can do with a degree in Geophysics. You may keep up with his writing and receive a free starter e-library by subscribing to his newsletter at: www.mlbuchman.com

Other works by M. L. Buchman: